# Starfish
# Feels Scared

Franklin Watts
First published in Great Britain in 2021 by Hodder & Stoughton

Credits
Series Editor: Sarah Peutrill
Series Designer: Sarah Peden

Every attempt has been made to clear copyright. Should there be any
inadvertent omission please apply to the publisher for rectification.

ISBN: 978 1 4451 7459 4 (hardback)
ISBN: 978 1 4451 7460 0 (paperback)

Printed in China

Franklin Watts
An imprint of
Hachette Children's Group
Part of Hodder & Stoughton
Carmelite House
50 Victoria Embankment
London EC4Y 0DZ

An Hachette UK Company
www.hachette.co.uk

www.hachettechildrens.co.uk

# THE Emotion OCEAN

# Starfish Feels Scared

by Katie Woolley and David Arumi

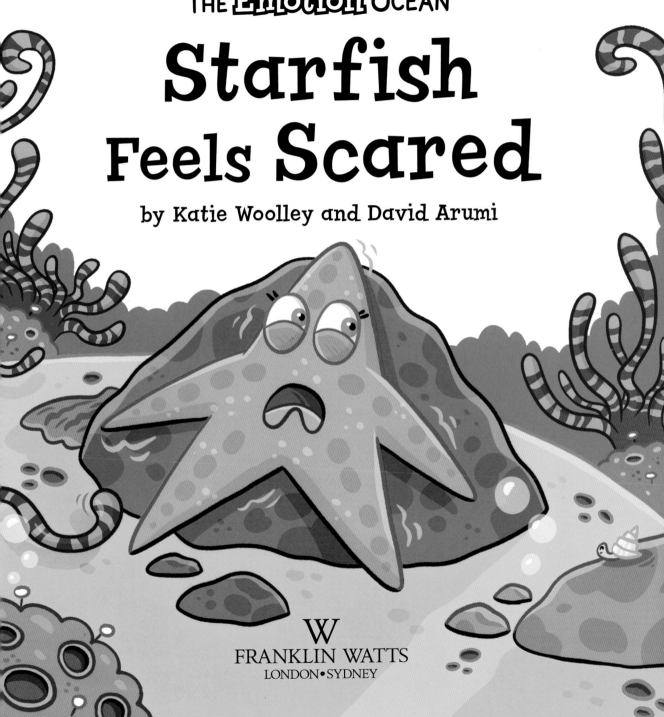

## W
### FRANKLIN WATTS
LONDON•SYDNEY

Class One were on a school trip to the play park.

Everyone was enjoying the waves, the bubbles and the surf.

Well, almost everyone ...

Starfish was stuck tight to a rock, watching her friends play.

"Come and jump with me!" laughed Jellyfish as he jumped on a **BIG** sea sponge.

"No thanks," said Starfish. "I'll get hurt."

Starfish wished she could be brave like Jellyfish, but it looked too scary.

Soon, all the other animals joined Jellyfish.

"Whee!" they cried. "This is fun!"

Starfish felt lonely and sad. But she didn't dare leave her safe rock.

Mr Narwhal spotted Starfish looking glum.

"Hello, Starfish," he said. "Are you having fun on the school trip?"

15

Starfish shook her head.

"I'm too scared to join my friends," she whispered sadly.

"We all feel scared at times," said Mr Narwhal.
"What is making you feel scared?"

"I'm scared I'll get hurt," Starfish whispered.
"I've never jumped on a sea sponge."

"New things can be scary," Mr Narwhal agreed. "But being brave and doing something new can be fun, too."

It does look fun.

"And sometimes what seems scary, turns out to be nothing to worry about," Mr Narwhal went on.

"I was scared the first time I swam on my own, but now I like it."

"I was sometimes scared of the dark!"
Starfish said. "But Dad got me a night light.
Now, night-time isn't scary at all!"

"Exactly!" cried Mr Narwhal. "I think if you can be brave, you will see that the sea sponge isn't so scary."

Starfish looked at her friends. She wanted to join in.

Slowly, Starfish lifted her feet off her safe rock.

She climbed onto the soft sponge and bounced up and down.

Then, she bounced <sup>up</sup> and <sub>down</sub> again!

In fact, Starfish kept on bouncing!

"Whee!" she shouted. "This *I S* fun!"

The next time Starfish felt scared, Mr Narwhal's words popped into her head and she was a little bit brave instead!

# Emotions are BIG!

Your feelings are a big part of you, just like they are a big part of Starfish and her friends. Look at the pictures and talk about their feelings. Here are some questions to help you:

Why did Starfish feel scared? What was she worried about?

What does Mr Narwhal suggest might be fun?

What did Mr Narwhal used to find scary?

How did Starfish's dad stop her feeling scared of the dark?

What does Starfish decide to try and do? Did she learn to be brave and have fun?

Have you ever felt scared to do something? What did you do to feel better?

# Let's Talk About Feelings

*The Emotion Ocean* series has been written to help young children begin to understand their own feelings, and how those feelings and subsequent actions affect themselves and others.

It provides a starting point for parents, carers and teachers to discuss BIG feelings with little learners. The series is set in the ocean with a class of animal friends who experience these big emotions in familiar, everyday scenarios.

## Starfish Feels Scared

This story looks at feeling scared, how it makes you feel, how you react to the feeling of being afraid and what you can do to overcome the emotion.

The book aims to encourage children to identify their own feelings, consider how feelings can affect their own happiness and the happiness of others, and offer simple tools to help manage their emotions.

## How to use the book

The book is designed for adults to share with either an individual child, or a group of children, and as a starting point for discussion.

Choose a time when you and the children are relaxed and have time to share the story.

## Before reading the story:

- Spend time looking at the illustrations and talking about what the book might be about before reading it together.

- Encourage children to employ a 'phonics-first' approach to tackling new words by sounding them out.

## After reading the story:

- Talk about the story with the children. Ask them to describe Starfish's feelings. Ask them if they have ever felt scared. Can they remember when and why?

- Ask the children why they think it is important to understand their feelings. Does it make them feel better to understand why they feel the way they do in certain situations? Does it help them get along with others?

- Place the children into groups. Ask them to think of a scenario when somebody might feel scared. What could that person do to make themselves feel better? (For example, they could take a deep breath and have a go or they could decide to do something else that isn't scary.)

- At the end of the session, invite a spokesperson from each group to read out their list to the others. Then discuss the different lists as a whole class.